ARNIE
and the New Kid

NANCY CARLSON

PUFFIN BOOKS

PUFFIN BOOKS
Published by the Penguin Group
Viking Penguin, a division of Penguin Books USA Inc.,
375 Hudson Street, New York, New York 10014, U.S.A.
Penguin Books Ltd, 27 Wrights Lane, London W8 5TZ, England
Penguin Books Australia Ltd, Ringwood, Victoria, Australia
Penguin Books Canada Ltd, 10 Alcorn Avenue, Toronto, Ontario, Canada M4V 3B2
Penguin Books (N.Z.) Ltd, 182–190 Wairau Road, Auckland 10, New Zealand

Penguin Books Ltd, Registered Offices: Harmondsworth, Middlesex, England

First published in the United States of America by Viking Penguin,
a division of Penguin Books USA Inc., 1990
Published in Puffin Books, 1992
1   3   5   7   9   10   8   6   4   2
Text copyright © Rufus Kline, 1990
Illustrations copyright © Nancy Carlson, 1990
All rights reserved

LIBRARY OF CONGRESS CATALOGING-IN-PUBLICATION DATA
Kline, Rufus.
Watch out for these weirdos / by Rufus Kline ; illustrated by
Nancy Carlson.   p.   cm.
Reprint. Originally published: New York : Viking, 1990.
Summary: Wanted posters introduce a gallery of offbeat characters,
including Erin "Starin" McCarron who looks in people's windows and
Bob "The Slob" McCobb who was once buried under the mess in his room.
ISBN 0-14-050907-0
[1. Humorous stories.]   I. Carlson, Nancy, ill.   II. Title.
PZ7.K6794Wat   1992   [E]—dc20   91-40899

Printed in Japan
Set in Zapf Book Light

For Barry...
who, just like Arnie,
teased someone and learned his lesson.

There was a new kid in school named Philip.

Philip was different from most kids.
He needed help doing some things.

Other times he didn't need any help at all.

Philip didn't have many friends at school.

No one knew how to play with a boy
in a wheelchair.

At recess Arnie would yell, "Let's race Philip!"
Of course Arnie would always win.

Arnie would tease Philip.
"Boy, do you eat slow," said Arnie.

One day after school Arnie started to tease Philip,
"Hey, look at me, I'm Philip!"

But Arnie didn't watch where
he was going.

"Ouch," cried Arnie.
"Call the nurse!" yelled Philip.

Arnie was rushed to the hospital!

A week later, Arnie came back to school.
He had a broken leg, a twisted wrist,
and a sprained tail!
Arnie needed help carrying his books.
It took him a long time to get anywhere.

At lunch, Tina had to get Arnie his food.
Arnie ate real slow. "It's hard to eat peas with
my left hand," complained Arnie.
Even Philip finished his lunch before Arnie.

During gym class Philip challenged
Arnie to a race. Philip won!

"Let me help you up, Arnie," said Philip.
"Boy, I could use a wheelchair like you!" said Arnie.

After school Arnie discovered Philip had
a huge baseball card collection.
Philip asked Arnie over to his house.
"Well, I don't know. What will we do?" asked Arnie.
"You'll see," said Philip.

Arnie had a ball at Philip's.
They played computer games all afternoon.

Soon Arnie and Philip were doing everything together.

After a few weeks Arnie got his cast off.
Arnie was so happy.

During lunch, Arnie ate so fast that Philip didn't
get a chance to talk to him.

After school Tina asked Arnie to play ball.
Arnie said, "On one condition...

"…as long as I can bring my coach."
"Sure!" said Tina.
And they all went to play baseball.